Between Here and Heaven

LUCINDA RACE

DEDICATION

Thank you to everyone who has believed in me and read each draft I've written and edited countless times. I dedicate this book to you.

Copyright © 2020 by Lucinda Race
Published by MC Two Press

Cover Design by Meet Cute Creative
Manufactured in the United States of America Second Edition
January 2020

E-book 978-0-9862343-4-7
Paperback- ISBN 978-0-9862343-5-4

CHAPTER 1

*C*ari studied the reflection of the calm, young woman in a long, creamy white, lace dress. The short cap sleeves enhanced sun-kissed skin; an antique pearl necklace graced the modest scooped neckline; and a wide, floppy, brimmed white hat with flowing lavender ribbons entwined waist length, wavy ebony hair. The reflection was picture perfect. Satisfied, Cari turned from the mirror and picked up her bouquet of cascading lavender roses and green ivy from the twin bed.

A rumble of thunder could be faintly heard in the distance. Cari glanced at the open window and hoped the rain would hold off until after the ceremony. She didn't want anything to mar this perfect day.

There was a light tap on the door. "Cari? Honey, are you ready?

Dad slowly opened the door. He saw his little girl standing before him in her wedding gown. He swallowed the lump lodged in his throat. "Where did my little tomboy go?

At a slender 5' 6", she looked like her mother. Her fine bone structure, high cheekbones, and a creamy complexion were framed by her long dark hair. Her emerald eyes sparkled, revealing every emotion.

"Oh, Cari. You look just like your mother did on our wedding day. I pray that you and Ben are blessed with a lifetime of happiness like we've had.

She could see Dad blink back a tear that threatened to fall.

He smiled at her. "I'm not going to be the reason you start crying before walking down the aisle."

Cari floated across the room to take her father's outstretched hand, the hem of her dress swishing as she moved.

"I love you, Daddy," she said as she kissed him on the cheek. With a nervous laugh she said, "Let's go get me married before my future husband gets tired of waiting."

Cari's heart skipped a beat as she saw Ben waiting for her at the altar. He was devastatingly handsome: the proverbial tall, dark, and handsome, with his tuxedo skimming his lean, muscular build. She could tell he was impatient for her to get down the flower-strewn aisle and become his wife. As she drew closer, she saw him take a deep, ragged breath, his deep blue eyes locked on hers. She had taken his breath away.

His best man, Art, poked him and whispered something to Ben. He nodded, speechless. He reached out to take her hand, and they turned to the waiting minister. As she stood on at alter holding Ben's hand she made a silent vow she would spend all her days making him happy.

The ceremony was a blur until the minister asked them to recite their vows. "Benjamin McKenna, do you take this woman, Cari Riley, to be your wife?"

"I do," Ben replied solemnly.

"And Cari Riley, do you take Benjamin McKenna as your husband?" "I do." Cari laughed in delight.

"By the power vested in me, I pronounce you husband and wife. Ben, you can kiss your bride." The minister gestured to Cari, and Ben was happy to oblige.

2

Applause rang out over the couple as Ben placed his hands on both sides of her face and pulled her in for the kiss to seal their marriage.

"Sweetheart, our life begins," he said for her ears only.

The remainder of the day whizzed by. Cari and Ben weren't sure if they had eaten or whom they had talked to, but the day was filled with love and laughter. They slipped away to change clothes before heading to their honeymoon on Cape Cod.

Cari twirled one last time in her dress before Ben undid the buttons and zipper.

"Ben, I can't wait until we get back and set up our apartment. It's going to be so much fun!"

He sat on the edge of the narrow bed, watching his new bride step out of the layers of petticoats and toss the dress over the vanity chair.

"Cari, you are so beautiful. Come here." His voice was husky.

Cari's heart hammered in her chest. She was beyond nervous. They had decided to wait until they were legally married before taking the final step in their physical relationship.

She slowly crossed the room to stand before him, barefoot, wearing a tiny slip….

His voice was husky. "Cari, you are so beautiful. Come here."

"Mom, where are you?" Kate's shouting jolted Cari back to the present. She slowly closed the cover on the wedding album and tucked the flood of memories back into the corners of her mind.

"In the sunroom!" Cari yelled.

Running footsteps sounded like a small herd of elephants on the hardwood floor. Kate and Shane, ten-year-old twins, and the baby of the family, Ellie, who was five, burst through the doorway, dropping their book bags next to the archway as they flew into the room. Ellie scrambled into her lap, placing butterfly kisses on Cari's cheek, not mentioning her tears.

Katelyn and Shane were almost identical and favored Cari. They both had dark, almost ebony hair, but Kate inherited her mother's amazing green eyes. Shane had his father's eyes, deep sapphire blue. They were both tall and slender, like Ben. Eleanor was tiny, with her mother's bone structure and complexion, but she had her father's eyes framed by sweeping dark lashes. Ellie may be a petite, little blue-eyed blonde, but the family resemblance to her siblings was undeniable.

"Hi, Mommy. What did you do today?" Ellie quizzed her mom.

Kate and Shane took up a spot on each side of the over-stuffed, floral chair. Before they sat down, Cari slid the album onto the footstool, making room for them.

"Well, I did the usual stuff—laundry, cleaning, gardening—and then I saw it was almost time for you to get home, so I took a minute to relax," she fibbed.

Cari smiled at each of them, trying to reassure them she'd had a good day. "And, now your home, so what would you like to do before we start homework?"

"Oh, we just got home. Do we have to talk about homework already?" Shane groaned. "My brain is stuffed and can't fit anything more into it."

Not to be left out, Ellie pulled her mom's arm. "Mommy, I don't have homework."

Kate glance at her bag on the floor. "Well, I have homework, but I was hoping we could make cookies or something and then work on it. Would that be okay?"

Kate was hoping she could talk her mom into doing something other than pretending to watch them do homework and drifting away from them. Cooking and baking used to make her happy, and she'd hum or sing, filling the room with the aroma of fresh baked cookies.

"I think that's a great idea. What would you like to make?" Cari was relieved they didn't want to go somewhere. She didn't have the energy to go to town or to the mall. It suited her just fine to hang out in the kitchen.

"Ellie, do you have an idea of what we should make?"

Cari waited patiently while the wheels in her little girl's head ran through her favorite treats.

"I think we should let Shane pick. He never gets to choose." Ellie turned and gazed up at her big brother. She idolized him and wanted to make sure he was included.

"Thanks, Pixie." Shane ruffled her hair, pleased that he was included. "We can make peanut butter balls. I'll do the measuring, Kate can mix, and then we can all roll them out and dip them in melted chocolate. Mom, you'll melt the chocolate for us, right?"

The kids looked at Cari, hoping she wouldn't say no. She waved her hands at them so she could get up.

"All right, peanut butter balls it is," she said as the kids pulled her into the large eat-in kitchen.

Kate was quick to put everyone to work. She had Shane clear the center island and pull out a stool, helping Ellie climb up and get settled. She gathered the bowls and other utensils she thought they would need. Cari settled onto a stool next to Ellie, while Shane put the radio on low for background music.

The kids were soon laughing as they squished peanut butter, crushed graham crackers and powdered sugar together with butter, and rolled the mix into small, misshapen balls lined on a cookie sheet. Cari melted the chocolate over a bowl of hot water and brought it to the counter so everyone could take turns dipping the balls in the warm, sweet, sticky, liquefied chocolate. Before all were dipped, Ellie was licking chocolate off her fingers, and Kate and Shane followed suit, so Cari finished the last few.

"Mom, how long before you think we can eat them? I don't mind being the taste tester," Shane smirked.

"Let's slide them into the refrigerator for a bit and we can check them later. When they're ready, we'll get some milk and have our snack. But let's clean up and get your homework started."

Cari's heart was a little lighter until she heard the clock strike half past four. She froze and then glanced at the back door expecting it to open. Each day Ben would come in with a big smile splashed across his face and arms open for his family to tumble into them. But he wasn't coming home today or ever again. It had been months since an aneurysm took him from his family. But Cari still expected him to walk through the door.

Kate, Shane, and Ellie stared at their mom as tears filled her eyes, threatening once again to dampen her cheeks. Cari took a deep ragged breath in an attempt to gain control. She couldn't cry in front of her kids. Not again.

"Let's get the milk poured," she said with a false upbeat tone in her voice.

The kids nodded as she retrieved cups, milk, and the tray from the refrigerator. She knew they wished their mom wouldn't be sad and cry every day. They missed their dad, too, but they didn't cry all the time anymore.

Shane touched his mom's arm as she gave him a glass of milk. His deep blue eyes looked squarely into her sorrowful eyes. "You're the best mom. Thanks."

Cari smiled at her son and pushed his dark hair from his eyes. She could tell he wasn't sure what just happened. She was relieved she did feel better today. They were starting to heal.

Looking at three sets of eyes looking up to her at that moment, Cari vowed her kids wouldn't find her sitting in a chair tomorrow when they got home from school. If she needed to cry, it would be in the shower. Cari was all they had left. She would be strong for them. Even if she had to fake it.

CHAPTER 2

The weeks flew by, and the holidays were fast approaching. Cari was dreading them without Ben. He had always made every holiday special, from Thanksgiving right through the New Year. How would she and the kids deal with the emptiness?

As Cari often did when the kids were at school, she sat in her chair in the sunroom, staring out the window crying softly.

"Cari, honey?" Ben's quiet voice reached her ears.

She turned to look at him standing next to the window overlooking the backyard. "Ben? Is it really you? I've had the worst nightmare. I thought I had lost you."

"Cari," he whispered, "it wasn't a dream."

"Stop. That's not funny. I can see and hear you," she insisted. "You couldn't have died."

"To be honest, the last thing I remember was someone in a white shirt kneeling over me as I lay on the cold hard ground. And the next thing I knew, I could hear you crying. It broke my heart, and now I'm here, standing in the sunroom." He paused, drinking in the sight of his beloved wife. "How long have I been gone?" His voice came in a hushed tone.

Cari felt tears start to well up. If he was real or just a figment of her imagination, she wasn't going to waste time choking back a sob when she could be getting some answers.

"It's been months since the policeman came to the door. You were walking through the store parking lot and, thankfully, you didn't know it happened. You were gone before you dropped to the pavement. You threw a blood clot to your brain." Cari paused, reliving the horror of those moments at the door. She swallowed hard, and continued. "It's been agony without you, but the kids are doing okay. At first, they were a mess. Ellie was afraid I would die too, and she was afraid to sleep alone. For weeks she'd creep into bed with me. Then the twins would come in, so the kids and I all slept in our bed."

She sighed. "Shane got into fights at school—nothing too serious, and usually with Jake, but that's stopped—and Kate withdrew into her books. But that's gotten better, too. The twins do a great job with Ellie, playing with her and helping out. Thankfully, school keeps them busy, but the holidays are coming fast, and I don't know how to do them without you." Cari stopped rambling and stared at her husband. "Ben, how long will you be here?"

"I don't know. I think your tears pulled me back to you." He waved his hand through the air. "Cari, we need to talk and figure out where you need to go from here. You can't spend your days sitting in the chair, staring out a window, watching the seasons pass. If you do, nothing will change on this side of the glass. You need to be strong for the kids, for me, and for you." Ben spoke in a gentle but firm voice. "You have to snap out of the depression that's suffocating you."

Cari struggled to maintain control over the emotions raging inside her. "Ben, you don't know what it's like to lose your other half and have to carry on for the kids. Each day I go through the motions of what's left of my life. What if I can't do this?"

"Honey, you don't have a choice. You're all the kids have —to lean on, to be their cheering section and their sounding board. I know you can do this for them. You were always there for me. But what are you going to do for you? You have to get out of this house for more than groceries or picking up the kids from school."

His face lit up. "What about baking? You know people are always looking for shortcuts around the holidays. Why don't you put up a poster at the market and offer breads and pies?" Ben waited for a few moments for the idea to register. "Cari, think about it. It's something you love to do, and you're good at it. You'll have a reason to get out of this chair." His voice softened. "I love you, honey."

Cari hung her head, ashamed that she had sunk so far into despair. Her mind went blank while she listened to Ben prodding her to take some action. When she looked up at him, the space next to the window was empty.

"Ben," she screamed, "where are you!"

Cari leapt from the chair and frantically searched the house, calling out for him around each corner. She entered the kitchen, grief washing over her again. She dropped on a stool. A well-worn pie cookbook lay unopened, as if waiting for her. She stared at it for what felt like hours when, in reality, minutes had passed. Hesitating, she dragged a legal pad and pen across the counter and opened the book. She hurriedly jotted a short list of five pies, dinner rolls, and quick breads. Satisfied, she turned to her computer and typed a brief announcement:

Pies, Breads, and Dinner Rolls

Let Me Bake for Your Holiday Gathering! Now Accepting Orders — Call Cari McKenna

Cari printed ten copies, grabbed them off the printer, and jumped in the car, quickly driving into town to hang the flyers before she chickened out. She retraced her steps home with doubts that anyone would place an order. Well, if she was going to do something, why couldn't it be something she enjoyed?

The kids bounded through the kitchen door, all smiles. With a chorus of "Hi, Mom—what's for snack?" they dropped their bags next to the back door and flopped around the kitchen table.

"Well, hello." She looked from Shane, to Kate to Ellie. "It looks like you guys had a good day. You're full of smiles." Cari felt her smile grow as she looked to her little loves. She couldn't help herself. Their mood was contagious.

"I have some news for you. I put up a few flyers around town, letting people know that if anyone didn't have time to bake, but wanted a pie or something for the holidays, to let me know. I don't know if anyone will place an order, but what the heck. It might keep me busy through the holiday season."

She looked at the kids, waiting for them to say it was crazy. She was surprised when Shane spoke up first. "Do you need official taste testers?" he said with a grin.

"I expect the three of you to be my official taste testers." Cari let out a sigh of relief.

A knock interrupted when Kate started to say something. Cari crossed to the door. When she pulled it open, her best friend, Grace Bell, was standing on the stoop, grinning from ear to ear.

Grace was a force of nature, full of energy and positive thinking. Tall and thin, with dark blonde, curly hair and soft brown eyes, some had made the mistake of assuming she was a pushover. They soon found out differently.

"So, you're going into the baking business. I want to be your first customer! I have to take a dessert to this dinner for Charlie's office, and you know I hate to bake. Heck, I can barely boil water!"

10

"Nice to see you too Grace." Cari closed the door after Grace entered the kitchen.

"I was relieved to see the flyers, and I'm going to do my best to drum up orders to keep you so busy that you won't have time to dwell." She dropped her shoulder bag on a vacant stool. "I'm even going to place one for myself."

"Grace, you're a nut. You don't have to place an order. I'll make whatever you need."

The kids greeted her with hugs.

Ellie tugged Grace's hand. "Gracie, do you want to have after-school snack with us?"

Grace looked into the sapphire blue eyes staring up at her. "How could I refuse? I would love to, Ellie."

She glanced over Ellie's head to Cari. "Remember that I'm a paying customer. Otherwise, I'll go shopping in the frozen food aisle at the grocery store."

Grace gave her a no-nonsense look, one that signalled Cari wouldn't be able to argue with her. Well, at least not in front of the kids. Cari held her tongue for now, but she wasn't taking money from her best friend.

"Well, I am happy to hear that the flyers are getting some attention," Cari murmured.

Grace gave her a silly grin. "The flyer was missing your phone number. Are you worried you'll get too many orders, or was it an oversight?"

"Honestly, I figured that the people who knew me will know how to find me, and I didn't think that anyone who didn't wouldn't want to place an order."

"Oh, it was deliberate. Well, in that case, I took the liberty of writing your phone number on the flyers I saw. Cari, you need to make it easy for people to place orders." Grace turned to wink at the kids as the phone rang, which, thankfully, didn't give Cari a chance to get mad.

"Hello?" Cari picked up the phone on the second ring. She paused, and then gestured for someone to hand her a pad and pen. "Yes, I would be happy to take an order. For Thanksgiving? Two pies—pumpkin and apple? You'll pick them up the Tuesday before the holiday? Perfect."

Cari jotted down contact information from the caller. She hung up and turned to Grace. "I guess you were right. I did need my phone number listed." Smiling, she tacked the order to the refrigerator. "So, who wants a snack?"

CHAPTER 3

*W*ithin a few days, the refrigerator was covered with scraps of paper that had detailed orders. Cari was trying to decide how to be organized and get everything made efficiently. She also wondered if she should stop accepting orders. Grace had been right: orders had poured in.

The Saturday before Thanksgiving, Cari got up very early and made a big breakfast for the kids. All of their favorites covered the table. She was going to need their help at the warehouse store to get the supplies she needed.

"Kids," she called up the stairs, "Breakfast!" She glanced at the clock on the wall. It was time they got going. The store would be open in about an hour and Cari wanted to get the shopping done so that she could start baking. Groans drifted down the stairs as her sleepyheads made their way into the kitchen.

Shane was scratching his head his hair standing on end and rubbing his eyes as he plopped at the kitchen table. He propped his head up with his hand, with eyes half closed. Mumbling he asked, "Mom, why do we have to get up so early? It's Saturday."

The girls weren't much happier at the early hour, but Ellie let out a squeal of delight when she caught sight of waffles with berry sauce and whipped cream sitting in the middle of the table.

"Oh, Mommy! Did you make the flat sausage, too?"

Shane opened one eye and really saw for the first time the table laden with waffles and all the special fixings. "What's the occasion? Somebody's birthday?"

"Well, it's a bribe. I need you all to help me today at the warehouse store. So, I thought if I made you a great breakfast that you wouldn't mind giving up your Saturday morning," she said hopefully.

"Jeez, Mom, you don't have to bribe us—we'll help. You know there are food samples too, maybe those really good cookies will be out again." Kate spoke with an overfull mouth of waffles.

Shane and Ellie were digging into the hot sausages and waffles. Ellie looked up at her mom. "Aren't you having some, too?"

"Of course, I am. I'm going to get a cup of coffee, so don't eat it all before I sit down." Cari chuckled softly as she poured a fresh cup. She wished Ben were here to see the kids jumping in to support her baking project.

A trip to the warehouse store was always an adventure with the kids. It was located in Everett, about fifteen miles from home. As she drove, Cari thought about how she had priced everything without any idea of what the ingredients actually cost. Hopefully she would break even at the end of next week, when everyone paid her.

As soon as they got to the store, Shane picked Ellie up, plopped her in the kid seat, and announced, "I'm pushing the cart!"

Ellie, small for her age, didn't mind sitting in the cart. This way, she got to see everything. Kate walked on the opposite side of the cart, picking up things as Cari read them off the never-ending list. From time to time, they would stop and get samples of juice, crackers, little pizza bites, and, best of all, warm cookies.

Piled high with baking items, Shane pushed the cart to the checkout line while Kate and Ellie waited patiently for Cari to pay. As they walked to the car, Shane and Kate poked each other, trying to get the other to speak up.

"Um, Mom, do you think we could help you with the baking or whatever, too? We think it'd be fun to spend the rest of the day hanging out."

Cari placed the items in the back of her SUV. "Shane, I thought you wanted to go over to Jake's?"

Jake Davis, Shane's best friend, lived on the street that ran parallel to theirs. Ben and Jake's dad, Ray, had cleared a wide path between the two yards when the boys were small so that they could easily run back and forth. Although the Davis' had lived there for seven years, Cari had never become friendly with Vanessa, Jake's mother. Most days, Vanessa was down-right rude.

"No. Jake and his dad are going to hang out together. Maybe I can set up the boxes and stuff you're going to put the food in. Or better yet, if we can stop at the office supply place and get some sticky labels, I'll make up some for the boxes. We learned how to do that in computer class. Then the boxes will be all ready when you're done baking."

Cari could see Shane's eyes sparkle with excitement. He seemed to want to help but cooking wasn't his favorite thing to do. She had to wonder if Shane noticed that she was happier since she had announced going into business.

Kate was nodding her head in agreement. "I want to help, and I bet there's stuff Ellie can do, too. Please, Mom? We really want to."

Cari looked at the three shining faces. She wouldn't dream of saying no.

"Of course, you can help me. We'll throw dinner in the

crockpot, and when we're ready, we can eat in front of the fireplace. Does that sound like a great way to end our busy day?"

Cari appreciated her sweet kids. Since Ben had died, they were ready to pitch in and help. She smiled to herself. They weren't angels, though. They still fought with each other like cats and dogs and didn't want to clean their rooms. Thank heavens they hadn't become Stepford Children. She didn't think she'd be able to handle that, too.

The kids all nodded and helped her finish loading the car. They had one more stop to make and a lot to get done before the day was over.

The four McKenna's piled the supplies in the middle of the oversized dining room table for easy access. It would be quicker to grab something than dig through the cabinets with the amount of orders that needed to be filled. Shane and Ellie worked on the label design for the dessert boxes and bags. Shane printed a sample to show her as Ellie clapped her hands in excitement.

Cari kept one ear on the kids. She held back a smile when she heard Ellie say, "Mommy's really going to like it, don't you think Shane?"

Shane nodded his head as he pulled the copy from the printer and passed it to Cari.

Cari's Homemade Delights

Cari smiled at the simplicity of the label. It was straight to the point.

"Go ahead and print them. What do you think of changing the color of the letters to dark purple? It will add a personal touch, since it's my favorite color."

Shane grinned and went back to the computer.

Cari listened as the printer shot out labels. Every one of

them would go on a box that held something she had created. She was surprisingly satisfied with the day as she measured flour and added a little salt to a large mixing bowl that held what would be the base for piecrust.

She drifted back to when she was a young girl about Ellie's age. Cari remembered watching her grandmother roll out piecrusts from a crumbled mixture that was stored in a large glass jar on the pantry shelf. Her gram would pour some into a bowl with ice water, quickly mix it up, and then roll it out on the floured counter. Cari knew this was a great timesaver in making the crusts for her orders, too. Once she was done with the base piecrust, she mixed the dry ingredients for the breads and rolls. All that would be left to do was combine dry and wet ingredients together and bake. Cookie dough was mixed and placed in containers in the refrigerator, also ready for the oven. As she mixed, she thought about how best to get everything baked and ready for delivery on Tuesday.

Cari surveyed the bowls on the counters and in the refrigerator, and sank her hands into the hot, soapy water to finish washing utensils while the kids dried. Exhausted, the four of them moved into the living room. The kids dropped to the floor in front of the fireplace as Cari lit the fire that she had laid out earlier.

Thank goodness, she had the foresight to put dinner into the crockpot. They would be able to eat whenever they had the energy to get up again.

"I think this was a very productive day. Tomorrow, we bake."

"Do we need to get up early again, Mom? I wanted to read a few more chapters of the Nancy Drew book I started last night."

"No, you can get up whenever. I'll get everything started. But I think we're going to have to skip our traditional Sunday breakfast. Maybe just cereal and toast, okay?" She waited a half second for a protest from them and rushed on to say, "I have a lot to get baked, wrapped, and boxed before the end of the day."

Mentally she made a quick note to put a list together with a baking order based on length of time needed and temperatures.

"Cereal and toast is fine Mom," Shane reassured her.

"Thankfully, tomorrow will be easier. If you want, hang out with Jake or ask him to come over."

Shane was quiet, thinking. "Yeah, maybe I'll have him come here. His mom doesn't like having kids in the house, unless we stay outside."

Cari couldn't understand Vanessa, but she'd decided a long time ago that it takes all kinds to make the world go around. "Ask him if he wants to work on your fort or something."

"Can we eat dinner soon? I'm starving." Kate interrupted.

"Let's fill our bowls and eat in front of the fire. It will be like we're camping and maybe, after dinner, I can find some marshmallows we can roast for dessert!"

Over the last several weeks, it finally hit Cari—the change was hard on all of them, but she was determined that someday they could look back and appreciate how they got through the darkest days of their childhood. The kids jumped up and raced to the kitchen to get dinner over with so they could have toasted marshmallows. Good natured shouting ensued for the best spot in front of the fire.

Quiet settled over the bakers as they inhaled dinner. Cari could hear the wind rustle and a tree branch scrape against the window. The weather had called for snow flurries. She hoped they wouldn't get much because she had neglected to find someone to plow the driveway. That was another thing in a long list of things that Ben had taken care of. Now it was one more item on her ever-growing to-do list.

Cari had rooted around in the back porch and found long shish kebob sticks, which were now holding large, white mounds of sweet, sugary treats currently stuck in the fire. Flames licked the marshmallows as they were transformed into balls of orange-blue flame. Ellie squealed with delight as she watched them become charred to a crisp on the outside, knowing they would be soft and gooey on the inside. One by one, they pulled the warm, sticky treats from the sticks and popped them into their mouths.

"This tastes just like summer," Ellie exclaimed. "Can I have another one, please?"

Cari pushed another one on Ellie's stick and helped her hold it up to the flame. Ellie reached up and patted Cari's cheek. "I wish Daddy was here. Don't you, Mommy?"

A lone tear escaped Cari's control and slid down her face. "Yes, baby girl. I wish Daddy was here, too."

Cari replaced the protective screen in front of the fire. Kate and Shane were quiet as they licked the remnants of marshmallow from their fingers. Ellie climbed into Cari's lap and snuggled her head under her mother's chin. For a time, they sat in silence, watching the fire dance.

The clock struck the hour and Kate yawned.

"Shane, help me clean up?"

They carried the sticks and bag of marshmallows into the kitchen. Cari could hear them teasing each other. She was relieved that, for tonight, they were fighting about loading the dishwasher.

Out of the corner of her eye, Cari saw the backyard flood-light come on. A large buck strolled into the yard, standing still and glancing around in the bright glow.

Cari quietly called the kids into the room. She pointed out the window at the deer.

Shane pulled at Kate. "Look, Sis, it's started to snow and see that huge deer!"

Cari and Ellie turned in the chair and stared at the little

flakes falling, a blanket of white on the grass. The buck stood as if waiting for everyone to witness his majestic bearing before slipping into the shadows. The winter season officially moved them forward. Life marched on.

CHAPTER 4

*C*ari slumped in a kitchen chair. Groceries sat on the counter waiting to be put away. She had delivered the last of the orders and stopped at the store to get food for Thanksgiving. She decided to make a traditional meal for her family. It was the first holiday after Ben's death, and she wanted it to seem as normal as possible. Her mom and dad were driving up from South Carolina to spend a week with them. They hadn't been back since the funeral. The kids were excited to see them, and it would break up what had become their new normal.

Cari hadn't cried as much since she started her baking business. It had gone well, and when she checked the numbers, she discovered there was a profit—not a large one, but it paid for the ingredients and her time. It was giving her something to think about for after the holidays. But for now, she needed to get through the next five weeks.

She glanced at the clock. The kids would be coming through the door in a few minutes, starving and looking for a snack. She got up and put the food away. Just as she finished, the kids tumbled through the door, full of high spirits. School vacation had begun, and for the next few days, all they needed to think about was playing and their grandparents would be coming for a visit.

Jake Davis was knocking on the back door as soon as the kids sat down at the table.

"Mom, I hope it's okay," Shane said as he pointed to Jake in the doorway. "His mom isn't home and his dad's working."

"Shane, you should have asked me, not that I mind when Jake comes over but next time please ask first."

She ruffled his hair as she walked by him to the cupboard to get a glass for Jake. "And don't spend the afternoon picking on your sisters."

She pulled out a chair for Jake and gestured for him to sit down. "Did you call your dad to let him know that you were here and leave your mom a note? I don't want them worrying about you."

He nodded. "I left Mom a note and called Dad's cell. He said he'd swing by and pick me up on his way home from work, if that's okay with you." He took a sip of milk and dropped his gaze. "You're really nice to me, letting me come over. My mom doesn't like me to have friends over very much."

"You're always welcome and if you want, stay for dinner. It's pizza night. Everyone gets to make their own, choosing their favorite toppings," Cari explained as she moved around the kitchen. Jake and Shane exchanged a quick look and grinned.

"Jeez, thanks. Count me in, I'm sure Dad will be good with it. Is it okay if I call him right now?"

"Finish your snack and put your dishes in the sink. Then you can call your dad."

Jake and Shane inhaled their cookie and took off for the family room. Before long, she could hear a video game at full volume and laughter floating into the kitchen. The girls were dawdling over their snack, looking unsure of what to do next. "What would you two like to do?"

The girls looked at her and thought for a minute. "Do you want to play a game or color?" Cari prodded.

"Can we play tea party?" Ellie looked between her mother and Kate, hoping they'd say yes. "It's a lot more fun with real people than with Teddy Bee and Suzie Dolly."

Kate rolled her eyes. It looked like that was the last thing she wanted to spend the afternoon doing. She gave a big sigh and looked at her little sister.

"Sure, pixie. Why don't we go set it up and call Mom when we're ready? Maybe you can dress up like a princess." Ellie's eyes grew round like big blue saucers.

"Oh, Katie, you're the bestest big sister in the whole wide world!" Ellie jumped up and grabbed Kate's hand, pulling her to hurry.

Kate flashed Cari a megawatt smile as she turned to follow the little girl up the stairs. Cari watched her two girls, blonde and brunette, make their way up the stairs. It amazed her at the contrast in their looks, but there was much love that flowed between them. The girls didn't know it at this tender age, but they were laying the foundation for a wonderful relationship as adults.

Dinner was a huge success. Jake enjoyed making pizza, and when his father came to pick him up, Ray thanked Cari for inviting Jake to stay. After the standard Happy Thanksgiving exchange, father and son walked across the back yard into the darkness of early evening.

"Okay, you guys. It's been a busy day, and its way past everyone's bedtime. Tomorrow is going to be even busier with preparations for Thanksgiving dinner and Grandma and Grandpa coming. Run along and get ready for bed. I'm reading a story, if anyone is interested."

"Mom, Kate and I are too old, but I'm sure Ellie wants a hear one," Shane informed her in the tone of a bored pre-teen.

"Okay, well, I'll be up shortly to tuck you all in." She turned, disappointed that it was going to be story time for one. The twins were growing up too fast, she thought to herself.

Kate popped her head in the doorway of Cari's room. "Ellie's all ready for bed, Mom." She headed down the hall to her room.

Cari crossed the hall and found Ellie sitting on her bed, cozy in PJs, snuggling with her stuffed bear, Ozzie. She had a fat book propped open waiting for Cari.

Cari kissed the top of her damp hair, inhaling the sweet scent of shampoo and soap. Silently, she thanked Kate for helping Ellie with her bath.

"Is that the book you picked? I think it might be longer than we have time for tonight. How about we pick out something a little shorter and maybe tomorrow we can read some of this book. Okay?"

"Mommy, then you pick a book that you want to read." Ellie set the book aside. "I'm so happy to have story time. I like it best when you make up stories, but you haven't done that since Daddy went to heaven."

Cari felt the vise constrict her heart a little. "Maybe we'll do a made-up story soon."

Ellie settled back into the pillows while Cari picked out Ellie's favorite book about a mouse that lived in a teacup. It was a book that Kate had loved when she was small, too. Ellie slid over and made space for Cari on the bed. Ellie's eyes grew heavy, and before the book was finished, she was sound asleep. Cari tucked her in, turned on her night light, and pulled the door halfway closed. Ellie had a habit of getting up early, just as the sun came up, and making her way into Cari's bed. Cari enjoyed these special moments, for soon it would be over. Kate and Shane had been the same when they were small. She took a last look and whispered, "Love you, pixie."

She walked down the hall to check on the twins. She

tapped on Kate's door first, easing the door open as she entered. The bedside light was on, book open, and her music played softly. Cari walked over and gave her a kiss on the cheek.

"Sleep well, sweetheart. Thanks for being such a good sport about the tea party and for taking care of Ellie's bath tonight. I was going to get to that in the morning."

"No biggie, Mom. A few bubbles and she's clean." Kate picked up her book, quickly becoming immersed in the story, but murmured softly, "Love you, too," as Cari pulled the door closed behind her.

Cari pushed Shane's door open with a knock, and he was laying in the dark, ready to sleep. Cari bent over to kiss him on the cheek. She couldn't do that to him in public anymore, but she could still get away with a goodnight kiss. "Goodnight, son. I love you. Sleep well." Cari turned and started to close his door.

"Mom? Are you doing okay? You know, with everything?" Shane sat up in bed, waiting for her answer.

"I'm good, honey. You don't need to worry about me. It's my job to worry about you. Grandma and Grandpa will be here tomorrow, and we'll have a good holiday. We'll have a few sad moments, but that's to be expected. Now, get some sleep. We have a busy few days ahead. Love you."

"Love you, too, Mom. G'night."

SHANE LAY back down in the comforting darkness and cried. He missed his dad. There had been times when he would catch his mom staring at nothing, lost in sadness. He didn't know how to help her, but he was the man of the house now. He'd talk to his grandpa, man to man. He would know how to fix everything.

He heard Mom go into her bedroom and firmly pulled the

door closed behind her. He knew she didn't want to take the chance that the kids would hear her cry again. Shane could tell she had been holding tears back all night. He tiptoed down the hall and dropped to the floor just outside her door.

The bathroom door opened and she turned the shower on. He guessed it was there, where the water would drown out the sounds of his mother crying. For what seemed like an eternity the water turned off. Next the sliver of light that peeked from under the door was gone. Still he waited. Listening. When all was quiet Shane made his way back to his room. Tomorrow would be better. It just had to be.

CHAPTER 5

*C*ari's parents pulled into the driveway and began unloading the car, as the kids rushed to get into coats before flying out the door to greet them.

"Grandma! Grandpa!" Three young voices in unison rang out over the crisp morning air. Cari watched the kids and her parents exchange hugs and kisses. She held herself back until her mother opened her arms and her daughter stepped into them.

A lump lodged in Cari's throat, and she had trouble eking out, "How was the drive?"

DAD WATCHED his wife and daughter. They could be identical twins, as they had the same eyes, hair, build, and coloring—beauties straight from the Emerald Isle. He could see the sorrow in his beloved daughter's deep green eyes. He noticed she was wearing her hair long, falling in waves, midway down her back, and it suited her. She was too thin, but with Sue around, he was sure they could get a few pounds back on her bony frame.

"Hello, baby girl," he whispered in her ear, wrapping her in a bear hug.

"Hi, Daddy." Cari lingered in his arms, inhaling his Old Spice cologne.

"I guess you didn't hit much traffic. We didn't expect you until after lunch." Cari motioned for the kids to grab a bag as she picked up the tote bag sitting on the frozen ground. "Let's go inside where it's warm," she turned and headed to the house.

Dave and Sue looked at each other over the kids' heads. After many years of marriage, they could communicate without words. Dave gave a slight nod. He understood their visit just got extended indefinitely.

THE PHONE WAS RINGING as the bags were dropped in the guest room. Cari picked it up. "Hello?"

"Cari, it's me, Grace."

"Hi, Grace. What time are you leaving for your parents?"

"Well, Dad has come down with the flu, and Mom said we should stay home because she's not going to cook a big dinner. So, I was wondering; could we invite ourselves to Thanksgiving dinner? I have pie!" she said with a laugh.

"We'd love to have you and Charlie for dinner. The more the merrier."

"That's perfect. Mom thinks Dad could pass this bug along and doesn't want us to get it."

Cari could hear Grace was trying to make this seem plausible.

"I think we'll eat at about two, but come over any time after noon. Mom and Dad will be thrilled to see you. It's been quite a while." Cari flashed back to the funeral. That would have been the last time her parents had seen her friends.

"Do you need me to bring anything else? Wine?"

"No, I'm all set. And, Grace, I'm happy you're going to be here for dinner. This means a lot to me."

Cari hung up the phone. I wonder if Grace's dad really is sick, but it doesn't matter. I'm grateful the house will be filled with people.

"CHARLIE, SHE KNOWS," Grace said as she hung up the phone and turned to her husband. "But you know I couldn't go to Mom's knowing that this was her first holiday without Ben."

Charlie pulled her into a bear hug against his broad chest, his head resting on the top of her soft curls. "Honey, it's what you do. You're her best friend, and you know she needs us, even if she won't say anything. So, we'll see our parents for Christmas, and Cari and the kids will spend New Year's Eve with us. We'll help her through the holidays." Charlie kissed her hard, thankful he had a sweet, caring wife.

THANKSGIVING DAWNED with a bright blue sky and crisp air. The family gathered in the kitchen, where the smell of turkey roasting greeted them as they came in search of breakfast. Cari was bustling around, peeling a mound potatoes and carrots while taking a sip from a steaming cup of coffee.

"Good morning, everyone." Cari had a large smile on her face. "There are some warm muffins and fruit salad on the table."

Sue looked around and saw that dinner seemed to be underway. "How long have you been up?"

"About an hour or so. I wanted to bake some muffins, and I had to get the turkey in the oven. I bought a twenty-pounder. I don't know what I was thinking. We'll be eating turkey for a month." Cari shrugged her shoulders with a

29

slight grin. "Mom, Dad, go eat," she said. "I'll be right over. I need to wash my hands."

The family was lingering over coffee and hot chocolate as the clock struck eleven. Cari got up and shooed the kids off to get dressed. Everyone had something to do, and there would be time to relax later. The kids needed to get the table set and the food ready.

Grace and Charlie arrived at noon, with Cari's pie, a bottle of wine for the adults, and apple cider for the kids. Hugs and Happy Thanksgiving wishes were exchanged around the room. Conversation flowed as overflowing bowls and platters were brought to the dining room. At one end of the table where Ben would have sat, Cari had placed a large flower arrangement instead of in the center of the table. No one said a word about the change in the tablescape. Once everyone was settled, Cari cleared her throat to say a blessing.

"Thank you for the people who surround our table today and for those souls who can't be with us." With a catch in her voice, she finished by saying, "Please don't let there be too much leftover turkey." She squeezed Grace's hand on her left and Shane's on her right. "Let's eat."

Dinner was devoured, and dishes were washed and put away. Feeling overstuffed, everyone adjourned to the sunroom and flopped on chairs and the floor. Dad was trying to convince Cari to play the piano, but she begged off, saying that she was too stuffed to move and didn't have the energy to get off the couch. The kids set up Scrabble, and Grace was helping Ellie spell words. The fun was contagious, and soon everyone was shouting out words for the board. Cari sat, enjoying the scene that was playing out in front of her, and realized she had gotten through the day without tears. She wished Ben was here with them—there was a void in the house today—but it hadn't felt empty. For the first time, Cari felt that she and the kids were going to get through this.

"Cari?" her mom interrupted her thoughts. "Would it be

okay if Dad and I stayed through Christmas?" Before Cari could object, she kept talking. "Your brother Justin is going to Lucy's parents, and it would be a long trip for you and the kids to come down to our place. So, if you don't mind, we'd like to stay around. It will give us a chance to spend more time with the kids and you."

"Mom, we're fine. You and Daddy don't have to babysit us. I know what you're trying to do. But we really are doing fine," Cari said in a hushed tone.

"Cari, wouldn't it be nice for all of us to spend Christmas together? It doesn't have anything to do with anything other than your father and me wanting to spend time with our grandchildren. So...is it okay?" she pushed.

Ellie was snuggled in her grandpa's lap, listening to the grown-ups talk. "Mommy, it would be fun to have Grandpa here. He can help us cut down our tree, and Grandma never made cookies with us. We can teach her how."

Seven sets of eyes rested on Cari. How could she say no without looking like a jerk? "Of course they can, Ellie. Mom, Dad, you're welcome to stay as long as you like. It's settled. But I hope you know it can be crazy around here on school days. I can't guarantee that you'll have any peace and quiet."

Dad laughed at her. "I think we can handle some noisy kids. We did raise a few of our own, remember?"

CHAPTER 6

The month of December flew by. Cari was surprised that people called in repeat orders and also had requests for Christmas cookies. It turned out to be a blessing that her parents stayed around. Cari needed extra hands to bake and deliver orders.

Cari and Mom were up to their elbows in flour, rolling out sugar cookies for an office party, when Mom brought up the baking business.

"I'm curious. What made you put up a flyer?"

"You wouldn't believe me if I told you," Cari said, shaking her head slightly from side to side.

"Sure I will. Try me."

The minutes ticked by while Mom waited for Cari to fill her in on the details.

"Well, this is going to sound a little crazy, but a few months after Ben died, he came to me, in the sunroom, and told me to stop spending every day in a chair, watching the seasons change. It was time I start living again. So, I put up a couple of flyers to see if there was any demand for baked goods for Thanksgiving. I was shocked when the orders started coming in. It was more like an avalanche. I needed something to keep busy, and it turned out to be a good diversion." Cari waited for her mother to be shocked at the revelation.

"Honey, sometimes we're given what we need, even if it's for a brief moment. My guess is you needed to talk to Ben. You two discussed everything. It's hard to recover from a loss. It's as if half of you was ripped away."

Cari was surprised that her mom seemed to understand. It helped her to feel a little less crazy. She was glad her mom knew about Ben.

"I haven't been able to talk to him again. I guess it was a one-time thing," she said sadly.

"Cari, don't look for him to come again. If he does, he does. I'm glad you decided to start a side business. You're a wonderful cook."

Mom slid a tray of cookies into the oven as she pulled another tray out. "I don't think I've ever wanted to not sample a cookie. This might be a great way to diet," she said laughing.

"Mom, I've had this idea running around in my head for the last couple of weeks, and I'm wondering if you'd give me your opinion. I've been thinking maybe I'll open a shop and make this a real job instead of a hobby. People seem to be willing to pay for my baked goods. I can make the hours work around the kids' schedules, and it would give us an income that would come in handy down the road."

Cari paused, letting the idea take root. After a long silence between the two women, Cari asked, "Mom? Do you think it's a bad idea?"

"Honey, I think that's a great idea it will give you something positive to focus on and additional stability. What do you need from us? We'd love to help you get started. Your dad is pretty handy with a hammer."

"I appreciate the offer, but Ben left us financially sound. I have the money to get started. Ben and I had talked about a shop when—well, you know—and he put money in an account for a start-up business. Anyway, it's something I'm thinking about. I haven't made any decisions. I'm going to wait and see what the New Year brings."

Cari abruptly changed the subject. "It looks like we have all the orders done, so I guess we should finish baking for us. Christmas will be here before we know it, and I still have shopping to do."

Mom was watching Cari flit around the kitchen, wiping down the counters and clearing away all signs of baking.

"Let's have a girl's day tomorrow. I think we've earned it. We can go shopping and out to lunch, maybe get our nails done, too. Dad will be here when the kids get home so we won't need to rush."

"It would be good to get the shopping done. Christmas is less than a week away. I'll let the kids know that Grandpa will get them off the bus tomorrow. I don't want them to worry."

"Great. I'll tell Dad that he's on his own tomorrow for the day." Mom cheerfully went off to find her husband.

CARI MET her mother in the kitchen bright and early the next morning. She didn't feel like going out, but it was something she'd do for her mom. Her parents had been very helpful the last several weeks, and Cari didn't want to disappoint either of them or give them a reason to worry about her.

"Good morning," Cari said to no one in particular as she walked in and went directly to the coffeepot. She was in need of a good dose of caffeine. She poured herself a large cup of the fragrant brew.

"Kids, remember that Grandpa will be here when you get home today. I know it's the last day of school, so please put your book bags in your rooms before you have a snack. Grandma and I will be home in plenty of time for dinner."

Dad jostled Shane's arm. "Your mom thinks we'll fall apart this afternoon."

"Yeah, I know. But we have everything under control, don't we, Grandpa?"

"We sure do, Shane."

Dad turned his attention to his daughter. "Cari when the kids get home today, we're going to go out to do a little shopping ourselves. So, if you try to call and there's no answer, don't worry. And then, tomorrow, we're going to all go pick out a Christmas tree. Is Snow's Tree Farm still open?"

Dad looked around the table at the kids as they smiled and nodded.

"Yes, they're open, and we usually get our tree there," Cari assured them all.

"Grandpa, can we be the first ones there tomorrow?" Kate wanted to know.

"Of course, we can, and we'll take a thermos of hot chocolate. It's thirsty work, picking out the perfect tree and all."

"That sounds like a great idea, Dad. Remember, you guys be good for Grandpa today, and remember to buckle up when you get in the car," Cari admonished them.

"Don't worry, Mom. We'll remember everything. You don't have to say it a zillion times!" Kate said. "We'll make sure Ellie is buckled up. Just have fun with Gram."

The kids hurried for the bus, anxious to get the last day of class over with, whispering to their grandfather on their way out the door.

"Dad, what was that all about?" Cari asked.

"Christmas secrets, my dear, Christmas secrets. Now, you and your mother run along. I'll hold down the fort for the day." Dad was doing his best to reassure his worrywart daughter.

CARI AND MOM finally made it to the mall in Everett. They

had made several trips to Cari's car, and it quickly became overloaded with bags of gifts.

Mom had been watching Cari go through the motions for the last few hours, and it was time for a break. "Are you ready for some lunch, Cari? I'd love to sit down for a little while and let someone wait on me."

"Sounds like a good idea. I could use something to drink. Shopping is thirsty work."

"So, now that we're alone, how are you holding up?"

"Mom, I have to do this for the kids, so I don't have a choice. I'll be glad when the last of the 'firsts' are behind me. I don't think that, after getting through the holidays, anything will feel this awful. I miss him so much. It's been almost eight months, but I still expect him to walk through the door every day. When will I stop missing him?" Cari hoped her mom had some answers.

"I think you'll always miss him. As time passes, it won't hurt as bad." Mom tried to comfort her as best she could.

"I guess when I think about it, the pain has dulled. But I wake up every day with an ache in my heart. I reach for the phone to call him and tell him something funny, but I remember he's not there. Instead, I find myself talking to him. Just like when I saw him in the sunroom. I guess talking to him helps, but I know it's crazy."

For the first time in a few weeks, she couldn't stop the tears from spilling onto her cheeks.

Mom placed her hand on Cari's, letting the silent tears work their magic. Cari needed to let her emotions out and not have them all bottled up.

"I know it's a cliché, but time does heal all wounds. Don't expect to wake up and suddenly feel like the old Cari before Ben died. This is the way you need to live your life. But while you're learning how to live without him, you have to think about three children. You're doing a great job with them and, for them. Don't be so hard on yourself. Your dad and I are very proud of how far you've come in these past months."

Cari didn't know what to say to her mother. She was happy to have her parents close.

"When are you and Daddy headed home?"

"Well, if it's okay, we thought we would stay until mid-January. Then we'll be back whenever you need us, or when we need a grandbaby fix. That's the good thing about retirement: we get to make our own schedule." Mom smiled at her.

Relieved that her parents weren't rushing off right after Christmas, Cari looked down at her lunch that was just delivered. "Mom, you and Daddy can stay 'til whenever."

Mom patted her hand. "Let's dig in. I'm famished!"

As they leaned back in the booth, Sue asked, "So, what do you think we should make for Christmas dinner?"

"I think we'll have a ham with all the fixings. The kids love ham, and then, during the week, we'll have sandwiches and scalloped potatoes with more ham." She grinned.

Cari pulled out a piece of paper and jotted down a few things they'd need. "We'll stop on the way home and get Christmas dinner fixings. Maybe if we're real lucky, we won't have to go back to the store for anything until after the holidays."

"It never fails. You think you've got everything, but there always seems to be one thing you forgot and that you can't live without," Mom said with a laugh.

CHAPTER 7

*L*ittle feet came running into Cari's room, and three bundles of energy jumped on her bed. "Wake up, Mommy! It's Merry Christmas Eve day!" Ellie shouted at full volume. "Santa's coming tonight!"

Cari opened her eyes to one set of dark green and two sets of sapphire eyes staring back at her. "Well, Merry Christmas Eve to you, too, my babies," Cari grinned. "What do you want to do today? Clean the chimney for Santa?" she joked.

Shane said, "Grandpa already did that. Ellie was worried that Santa would get his suit dirty, so instead, let's have breakfast first, and then maybe we can build a snowman. We have lots of snow 'cause it snowed hard last night!"

Enthusiastically agreeing with him, Kate piped up, "Let's go fix breakfast for Mom!" They climbed off the bed and headed for the bedroom door. "Give us fifteen minutes, okay?" Kate demanded.

"Don't worry, Mom. We'll even clean up." Shane pulled the door firmly shut behind him.

Cari chuckled to herself as she got up and went into the bathroom to get ready for the day. Kate was a little bossy this morning, but it was sweet of her to take charge of things. Cari peered at her reflection in the mirror and could see faint lines around her eyes. Where did they come from, she wondered? She leaned into the mirror for a closer look.

"I guess it's nothing a good facial cream won't fix."

She ran a brush through her hair, put a few swipes of mascara on her lashes, and was ready to head downstairs. She must have wasted enough time fretting over new wrinkles for the kids to have cooked breakfast.

At the bottom of the stairs, she could hear laughter drifting out from the kitchen. It was music to her ears. It had been a long time since the house had been filled with laughter. She walked through the door and stopped dead in her tracks. Laid out was a feast, complete with flowers on the table, cloth napkins, and her good china.

Mom and Dad were supervising the small kitchen crew and didn't see Cari standing in the doorway. Ellie saw her and ran over to grab her hand, tugging her into the room.

"Come on, Mommy, wait 'til you see what we're eating! Katie and I made the menu. Grandma helped Shane and Katie cook and, Grandpa and me, we set the table. Do you like it?" Ellie was looking up at her mother, her rosy cheeks shining. Her smile couldn't get any bigger.

"My goodness, you have been busy. The table looks beautiful, and it smells wonderful in here. What are we having?

"Scrambled eggs with bacon, toast, and chopped fruit," Kate proudly announced. "It's ready, too."

Ellie pulled her to the table and said, "Sit next to me, please?" Cari slid onto the chair and waited while Shane delivered her coffee.

When everyone was seated around the breakfast table, Shane cleared his throat.

"We hope you were surprised and that you like everything. And it's one of your Christmas presents."

Cari was touched at their thoughtfulness. "You couldn't have given me anything I'd like more. After breakfast, and when the dishes are done, everyone needs to put on warm clothes—we have a snowman to build!"

Time flew, and soon there was a family of snowmen standing on the front lawn. Grace and Charlie pulled in just as Ellie was demanding hot chocolate.

Cari greeted her friends. "Hi, guys. Want to join us for cocoa? We've been outside for hours, and our fingers and toes are frozen."

Grace looked at Charlie. "Sure, we can stay for a little bit, and then we're headed out to the family's," Charlie said.

Everyone stripped off their wet clothes as soon as they got into the house. Cari directed the kids where to put them while her Dad got a tray of cookies for the table, and Kate and Ellie got out the mugs.

"You look good today, girlfriend."

Cari smiled and it wasn't the forced smile she had been wearing for so long.

"I'm doing pretty good today. For the first time in a long time, I felt good when I got out of bed. I don't know how long this will last, but for today, I'm going to enjoy being happy. We're going to have a picnic in the living room tonight, cook hot dogs over the fire, and then watch a holiday movie. I'm hoping the kids will be tired enough to go right to sleep. Santa comes tomorrow, and I know it's going to be a good day."

Cari looped her arm through Grace's. "You don't need to worry about me, you know. I'm better. I still miss him like crazy, but we're all going to be okay."

"I'm glad, Cari. I know you have good and bad days, but I was worried about today. I'm glad we stopped over. I don't think we need to worry about you, at least for right now."

Cari gave her a fierce hug. "Grace, I know you'll continue to worry but I'm coming out of the long, dark tunnel."

Grace and Charlie left about a half hour later with promises to call and talk about plans for New Year's Eve.

Three generations waved from the porch as the car pulled away. Cari ushered everyone back into the warm house.

"What do you think? Should we start our movie early?"

A chorus of happy voices screeched, "Yes, let's build a fire and get the living room ready for our Christmas Eve party!"

The kids were right on their mom's heels, with Mom and Dad following at a leisurely pace.

CHAPTER 8

After a relaxing evening in front of a roaring fire, Cari tucked the kids into bed, and her parents retired to their room. She had read the traditional Christmas story and was sure visions of treats and treasures were dancing in their heads. They would be up early tomorrow to see what Santa had left them.

She said goodnight to her parents and wandered downstairs to sit in the glow of the tree, revelling in the silence that crept over the house.

Every year, she and Ben would sit and enjoy looking at the tree with the gifts surrounding it. Cari needed to keep this tradition alive.

"Oh, Ben, I wish you were here tonight. The kids have been so good—well, most of the time—and they've loved having Mom and Dad here. I'm thinking about opening a small shop and really jumping into business with both feet. I've enjoyed the process of meeting with people, taking orders, and then seeing their happy faces when I make the delivery." She sighed and closed her eyes, wishing Ben knew that she was in a better place.

"I always knew you could do it, Cari." Ben was sitting on

the sofa, looking exactly the same as he did when he had stood next to the window.

"You're here...." Cari said with a catch in her voice.

"I've wanted to check on you and see how things were going, and tonight seemed like a perfect time. Since the first time here, I've found a way to keep my eye on you and the kids. I see you're all doing much better. The twins are acting more like preteens, which is a double-edged sword," he said with a low chuckle.

Cari couldn't take her eyes off Ben, lost in the precious moment.

"Do you remember when we had the twins and we were so sleep deprived? We hadn't had a minute of downtime since we brought them home. It was Christmas Eve, and it was the first time in weeks that the kids were sleeping at the same time. We sat in the living room with the lights on the tree and enjoyed a glass of wine. Remember? We got to sit and talk to each other without a crying baby between us."

"I remember," Ben smiled.

"Oh, I miss those days. We were so young, and with two babies." Cari shifted from the past to the present. "How long can you stay with me tonight?"

"Not long. But I wanted to come and wish you a Merry Christmas and tell you how proud I am of you and how much I love you. I knew you'd do a great job pulling everyone together."

Cari felt the warmth of his love wrap around her.

"Since you're here, can I bounce my shop idea off you? You know I haven't made a major decision in the last fifteen years without talking it over with you first."

"I'd like that." Ben leaned forward as Cari outlined her plan for opening a shop. She told him what items she thought she could sell, and that it would be open for breakfast and lunch four days a week.

"I don't want to short-change the kids, so I'll spend four

days at the shop to start with, and they can come, too, if they want. It will be a family project." Cari finished and waited for Ben's advice.

"Wow, you've got a sound plan. You're going to need a contractor. Whatever space you rent will need counters, shelves, and stuff. Talk to Ray Davis. He's good and fair. He won't take advantage of you. Also, at some point, plan on buying the space. Don't be a renter forever. Build equity into your business. Don't wait too long before getting started. Maybe you could be open by Easter."

Cari relaxed—Ben liked her plan. It felt good to lay it out for him. Like always, he was a great sounding board. Cari leaned back in the chair and yawned.

"Things are getting better, but I miss you like crazy. It's been so hectic the last few weeks. I guess I'm more tired than I thought."

"Why don't you go up and get some rest?" Ben suggested.

"I don't want to waste a minute of time with you. I'm going to close my eyes for one second so I can burn the picture of you sitting next to the tree in my memory."

Ben blew her a kiss as she closed her eyes. When she opened them, Ben was gone. Again.

Dejected, Cari sank into the sofa cushion, staring at where Ben had been only moments before. She could swear she smelled his aftershave in the air. She dropped her head into her hands, wanting to cry, but strangely enough, the tears didn't come. If this was all she was going to have of Ben—the occasional conversation—then she'd treasure each conversation. If that were all she was going to have, it would have to be enough. Sighing, she took a drink of the milk and nibbled a cookie that the kids had left for Santa. Morning would come quickly, and the children would be awake extremely early. Maybe if she was lucky, the sun would have started to come up.

Cari stood, looking around the room. "Goodnight, Ben. I love you."

CARI WOKE WITH A JOLT. It was morning and the kids weren't up yet? The sun was streaming shades of pink and red in her bedroom window. She bolted out of bed, slid her slippers on, and grabbed her robe on the way out the door. The kids' doors stood open and beds were empty. What on earth was going on? Why didn't anyone wake her up?

Cari raced down the steps, not having any idea of what she may have slept through. She heard voices in the kitchen and made a detour from the living room where the tree had unopened gifts sitting beneath the green branches. Stopping short in the doorway, she found her children and parents making breakfast. No one was clamoring to get to the presents. Were these her children?

Everyone calmly looked up, as she stood there, stunned. "Well, good morning sleepy head," her mom said. "We thought you weren't going to ever get up. The kids needed something to do, so we decided to cook breakfast."

Kate and Ellie walked over to hug Cari. "Well, this sure is a nice surprise!"

"Don't get too excited, Mom. It's cold cereal and juice with coffee and hot cocoa. We can't stand the waiting and want to eat fast. Did you see what Santa left under the tree? Ellie doesn't think he went to any other houses and that he left all the presents in his sleigh here." Kate ran her hand over her little sister's blonde curls.

"Well then, I guess we had better take our breakfast and go open stockings while we eat. No sense in keeping everyone in suspense any longer."

Cari was eager to have the kids open their gifts. Later today, she was going to talk to them about her shop and see what everyone thought. Maybe over vacation, they could look at empty storefronts.

Before the words finished leaving her mouth, the kitchen was empty and everyone had found a spot near the tree.

Cari leaned back in her chair, surveying the piles of paper that lay around the room. Ellie was talking to her new doll, Kate had her nose buried in the first book in a new mystery series, and Shane was working alongside Grandpa, setting up his new video game system. Mom walked into the room with two mugs of fresh coffee, passing one to Cari as she stepped in front of her on her way to the sofa.

"I guess we can say the gifts are a hit," she said as she glanced around the room at the happy kids.

"I think that's an understatement, Mom." Cari was smiling when she caught her mom looking at her.

"You seem good today, honey. Did you sleep well last night?"

Cari dropped her voice to just above a whisper. "Ben came to see me last night. We got to talk for a long time. I've come to the conclusion that if I get to see to him from time to time, it's better than never talking to him. So, I'll take it."

"I think it helps you to talk to him, soak up what you can and don't worry about the rest." Mom agreed with her.

"You're right. I woke up today feeling better than I have in a very long time. I think seeing him and telling him about the shop helped me get ready to take the next step. I'm going to talk to the kids after we have dinner and see what they think."

Cari nodded in the kid's direction. "See how happy they are? I think when I'm okay, they're okay."

"Cari, you're their world, their rock. The stronger you are, the stronger they'll be. You won't ever stop missing Ben, and neither will they. But you'll move on." Mon got up to head into the kitchen. She placed her hand on Cari's shoulder and gave it a squeeze. "I'm very proud of you."

CHAPTER 9

*C*ari and the kids were waiting outside the vacant storefront on Main Street and Castle, directly across from the town park. Cari decided it was the perfect location for a coffee shop. She had asked Ray Davis to meet her there to look it over before she signed the lease. She negotiated with the option to purchase the building within the next two years, and she was confident it would work out. In her mind's eye, she could see an eclectic bunch of tables and chairs filling the room, inviting people to come and linger over coffee and something to eat. On a nice day, people could take their coffee and sit in the park. She had been playing around with the menu, and before she went overboard, she had to confirm the building was worth sinking time and money into it. She didn't need a money pit.

RAY DAVIS PARKED his truck across the street. It had been a rough few weeks, but he wasn't ready to talk about it. Vanessa, his wife of fifteen years, up and left him and Jake. She didn't want to be a wife and mother, so all Ray and Jake had left was each other. He would deal with the pain, and Ray would be both mother and father to his son. He watched Cari blossom as she handled both roles with dignity, grace, and strength. At some point, he'd confide in Cari. Jake would need his friend Shane to adjust to the changes ahead. But, for now, Ray had a job to do.

Ray jogged over to Cari and the kids as she gave him a big wave.

Shane stretched out his hand. "Thank you for coming, Mr. Davis. We hope you can help us get 'What's Perkin?' open by Easter."

CARI SMILED as her son and Ray talked about the shop. He seemed to have grown up overnight. Mother's intuition whispered to her that this new business would be just what they needed to move forward with their lives. Who knew what would happen next? Cari shivered with excitement, ready to face a future full of possibilities.

The End
Keep reading for a sneak peek at:
Lost and Found- Book 2 The Loudon Series

CHAPTER 10

*C*ari peered through the rain-covered windshield. The wipers thudded as they slapped from side to side. Her headlights barely illuminated the road ahead. The humidity hung heavy with the threat of bad weather. A nasty storm had barreled through and deluged the area just as she had closed the shop. She should have taken the weatherman seriously when he'd predicted severe weather earlier that day.

Her stomach tightened with each rumble of thunder. Suddenly, a bright bolt of lightning lit up the sky and seemed to strike something just beyond the tree line. She had never been a fan of storms, and it seemed they'd grown more severe lately. Maybe there *was* something to climate change.

Her street was ahead, and relief coursed through her. The road was inundated with water. Lightly tapping the brakes, she turned left onto Maple Lane. The sky was as black as night and the lampposts went dead and the street was plunged into darkness. Anxious to get home, she drove slowly avoiding the debris and dodging the tree limbs that bent low, kissing the ground. The bright headlights swept over the driveway as she pulled up to the garage door. She waited impatiently for it to open wide enough to get the car stowed inside. "Oh shoot. No electricity."

Cari parked the car in the downpour and dashed to the back door, firmly slamming it behind her. Leaning against it, she took deep breaths to steady her hammering pulse as the hair on her arms stood on end. A thunderous crack rang out, immediately followed by a large bolt of lightning illuminating the kitchen. Oh, no, she thought, realizing what had been struck was very close to where she stood. She felt the house shudder and then—deafening silence.

She pulled herself together and crossed the room. As she peered out the kitchen window, she was shocked to discover that the large pine tree, which had dominated the backyard for the last twenty-five years, was now resting on the roof of her house. It had split down the middle and hefty chunks of the trunk and branches covered the ground. She made her way to the sunroom at the back of the house. It was in shambles. Shards of glass and wood splinters littered the floor. Stunned, she stared at the carnage as the sun broke through the dark, heavy cloud cover.

"For crying out loud, Ben. Look at what your stupid tree did! I told you not to plant it so close to the house. Your tiny tree grew into a monster." The ghost of her late husband didn't answer her.

Cari stalked to the backdoor and flung it open. She stepped into the heavily pine-scented air. For a brief second, she inhaled deeply, savoring the cool, fresh air the storm had left after washing away the oppressive heat.

"What are we going to do?" She gingerly picked her way through the branches that peppered the lawn. "The back side of the house is devastated." Tears filled her eyes. "I'll call Shane. This mess needs heavy equipment. I'm sure he'll bring the guys over to clean it up."

She was surveying the damage and muttering to herself

when her neighbor, Ray Davis, came over. Hopefully he hadn't witnessed her yelling at the tree from his window.

He cleared his throat. "Ah, Cari, are you okay?"

She was relieved to see him standing less than three feet away from her. Hopefully, he hadn't heard her talking to herself. At six-foot-three, he towered over her. She jammed her hands into her front jean pockets.

"Hi Ray, did you hear me talking to myself?"

He gave her a sheepish grin. "Actually, I could hear you yelling at the tree. I thought I'd come over to see how I could help."

Gesturing to the pieces of the tree that lay before them, she said, "Well, I guess my day ended with a bang. This little seedling Ben planted decided it didn't want to be in the rain, so it came inside the house. Unfortunately for me, it didn't come in as firewood," she said ruefully. "A couple of years ago, Shane wanted to cut it down. But, no, I had to be stubborn. I told him there was no reason to take it down because it was healthy. In hindsight, I guess I should have listened to reason. I just didn't want anything changed in the yard."

"Hey, don't beat yourself up. No one knows when or where lightning will strike—it just happens. Have you called your son yet? I can stick around and give him a hand. But we should drape a tarp over the hole in the roof before it gets dark."

"That's so nice of you to offer, but I don't think I have one large enough. This is so frustrating! I can't believe it happened."

"I've got a tarp in my shop you can use until you figure something out. I'll run over, get it, and be right back." He jogged across the adjoining yards to get it.

Pulling her cell phone out of her back pocket, she pushed a number on speed dial. Trying her best to sound casual, she said, "Hi, Shane, its Mom. Wasn't that a doozy of a storm?"

"Hey, Mom. Everything is fine here at the lake, but it was pretty bad!"

"That's an understatement. Any chance you can swing by?" Cari paused. "Before you say, 'I told you so,' I need to tell you something."

"Okay, what's going on?"

She could hear the concern in his voice and was sure he knew why she called. It was just a matter of time before a storm brought down the pine tree.

"Remember that large pine in the backyard, the one you told me needed to be cut down? Well, it got struck by lightning, split down the center, and crashed onto the house."

"The tree got hit?" He let out a low whistle. "How bad is it? Should I call Don too?"

"No, don't bother your brother-in-law tonight. Ray was here and just left to get a tarp to cover up the gaping hole. But you're going to need a ladder." Cari stated flatly while staring at the roofline.

"All right. Hang tight, and I'll see you soon." Shane abruptly disconnected without saying goodbye.

Cari went into the kitchen to grab cold drinks. She and Ray might as well be social while waiting for Shane. She was fortunate to have a good neighbor. He was always willing to lend a hand when needed. She dealt with her loneliness most days, but at this second, she missed her husband more than ever.

Her eyes followed Ray as he made his way back to the deck. He was all male, and the proverbial tall, dark, and handsome variety. His features were strong and sharp without being harsh. They were enhanced by dark hair, peppered with a touch of gray that swept down over cool blue eyes that a girl could easily drown in. Why he didn't have a girlfriend was beyond her. There must be at least one woman in town looking for a nice, divorced man. Trotting next to Ray was Gifford, a fifty-pound ball of fur whose tail was always wagging. Gifford turned up on Ray's back step one day, and he adopted the pup on the spot. Now, the two were inseparable.

Ray carried a huge, blue plastic bundle in his arms. "Here's the tarp." Gifford dropped to the ground and promptly started a gentle dog snore, exhausted from the long walk across the yard.

"That's overkill; isn't it?" Cari joked as she handed him a cold beer.

"You're kidding, right? Did you see the huge hole in your roof? I'm worried it won't be big enough!"

"I'm trying to be a little more optimistic." Cari was saddened to see the devastation of her beloved home.

She watched Ray take a slug of his beer. She sipped her own and wished Shane would hurry up. Thankfully, it wasn't long before his truck appeared around the side of the garage, coming to an abrupt stop on the lawn. Climbing out, Shane took in the full extent of what had happened. He crossed the lawn, eating up the distance between them. He was the spitting image of his father—long, lean, and muscular—but had inherited his mother's dark hair, his father's blue eyes, and a quick, easy smile. By twenty-five, he'd established a reputation in the community for his honesty and hard work with his landscaping business. He worked side-by-side with his crew at every site, getting the job done safely and on time. Cari was proud of her only son.

Shane extended his hand. "Good to see you, Ray. Did you see the tree crash or just hear Mom yelling at it?"

The men chuckled.

"This isn't funny, and I don't appreciate that you two are laughing at my expense." Immediately Cari became contrite. "I'm sorry. I'm mad at myself for not listening to you, son."

"Mom, I'll take the blame on this. I should have insisted

you take the tree down before now. I knew we were on borrowed time. I understand you and Dad planted it to commemorate buying the house, but now it's going to take some serious work to get everything cleaned up and the house fixed."

Shane softened his approach. "I know this hurts. Let's go see how bad it is and then get the tarp slung over the hole as best we can. Tomorrow, we can get things moving."

Cari watched as Shane and Ray checked out the mess from all angles and discussed the best way to get the tree off the house without additional damage to what was left of the structure. She trailed along behind the guys, wishing she had listened to her son years ago.

She couldn't help but stare at the tree branches jutting out from the glassless windows.

Under her breath she murmured, "What a mess this is. I can't imagine how much money it will take to fix it."

Cari stomped into the house and slammed the back door harder than she had intended. She grabbed a beer for Shane and went back outside. It gave her a couple of minutes to pull herself together. The guys walked toward Cari with Gifford at their heels.

Taking a deep breath, she prepared herself for the bad news. "Any possibility we can get the tree off the house tonight? I hate the idea of being exposed to whatever little critters and wiggly things that might find their way inside."

"Mom, I'm sorry. The best we can do is drape the tarp over the roof. I can have my crew here bright and early tomorrow. You should get pictures before the sun sets for the insurance company. Tomorrow morning, the guys will get the tree off the house and clean up the debris. Don and I will come back to get the logs cut up for firewood. It's not safe to do anything more tonight."

Frustrated, Cari shrugged her shoulders. Shane retrieved the extension ladder from his truck, setting it against a solid wall of the house. Ray handed up a side of the tarp and together they pulled it over the gaping hole. She watched as Shane stole a glance at her. She could guess what he was thinking. Patience wasn't one of her virtues.

RAY COULDN'T TAKE his eyes off Cari. Despite the current situation, her beauty struck him. Shining emerald green eyes were fringed with long, dark lashes. Auburn streaks highlighted her ebony hair, which framed her delicate features. She could stop a man in his tracks, he thought.

Ray wanted to help and as a contractor he didn't want her to be taken advantage of either. "Cari, I can give you the names of a few good contractors. The insurance company will request several estimates. If you'd like, I can give you a quote for repairs; it will give you something to compare with the other estimates. I'm happy to explain any terms you're not familiar with. Just give me a shout."

Ray's gentle tone seemed to soothe her raw emotions, as he noticed her expression start to relax.

"I guess I don't have a lot of choices at the moment. I'll have to be patient until everything is cleaned up. Thank you for being so understanding. You've been so nice about all this. I really do appreciate your help."

"I'm going to head home, Mom. Try not to worry about everything tonight. Tomorrow is another day." Shane hugged his mom tight. "Get some rest."

"Cari, if you're all set, I'm going to take off, too. Unless you need something, and then I'm happy to hang around for a while longer." Ray wasn't in a rush to leave, but he didn't have a good excuse to stay.

"No, I'm all set. Thanks again, Ray, for everything. You were a big help tonight. I'll see you tomorrow at the shop?

Breakfast is on me. After all, it's the least I can do." Cari gave him a lopsided smile.

"You don't need to buy me breakfast, but thanks. I'd never miss out on your cooking," he teased. "Good night, Cari." With a jaunty wave, he went home. As he walked through the door he could see Cari. Her shoulders were slumped as she walked into her house.

SHE FOUND herself inexplicably drawn to what was left of the sunroom. Standing on the threshold, she peered into the gloomy darkness from the long shadows cast by the tree. Scanning, she could see her piano on the other side of the room. Unsure of its condition, she picked a path over the debris and, to her delight, discovered the old baby grand and her treasured family photos sitting atop it were in pristine condition. The cushions on her overstuffed chair and ottoman were littered with pine needles, but otherwise untouched. Ben had given her the set when Ellie, her youngest daughter, was born. She was amazed at the total destruction on one side while the other remained untouched.

The ivory keys called to her, willing her fingers to lovingly caress them from rich low bass tones to sweet high notes. She studied the photos on display. Frozen moments of a full and happy life: a wedding photo with Ben and one with their newborn twins, Kate and Shane. She reached out to study a picture of the twins tucked into a chair and proudly cradling Ellie the day she came home from the hospital. She could still hear Kate tell her that baby Eleanor looked like a pixie, with wispy blond hair and crystal blue eyes, long eyelashes, and deep dimples. She had begged Cari to rename her Pixie Dust. She and Ben had laughed it off, but the nickname stuck.

Cari set the picture down. She continued her journey down memory lane until her eyes came to rest on a framed photo. She, Ben, and the kids were grinning, despite the cold. They were gathered around a freshly-cut Christmas tree. It turned out to be their last trip to the tree farm as a family. The smiling faces in the photo weren't prepared for the heartache to come the following spring when five became four.

Cari dropped to the bench in front of the keys. Unaware of what she would play, her fingers found a melody. Raw emotions bubbled up from the depths of her soul. Slow and thick with emotion, music began to drift to the heavens.

Cari played music late into the night as a feeling of peace enveloped her. She glanced up through what used to be the roof. Pinpoints of light dotted the heavens. Hugging her arms tight around her against the chilly night air, she made a wish on the stars. Turning on the polished wooden bench, she took one last look around the room. Countless moments—wonderful, bittersweet, and heart-breaking—had all taken place within these walls. Cari knew it was time for changes that went beyond paint on the walls and new curtains. Rebuilding would be the first step in making a fresh start, but there would need to be significant change. Cari decided to speak with Ray tomorrow. She wondered what could be possible without changing the footprint of the house. Exhaustion invaded her weary bones. New ideas would have to wait until tomorrow. Without a backward glance, she left the room and crawled up the stairs. Sliding between the cool sheets, drained, she fell into a dreamless sleep.

SOFT NOTES WAFTED over to Ray, sitting in the dark on his patio. The melody tugged at his heart. In his mind's eye, he could see tears sliding unnoticed down Cari's cheeks. There had been countless nights when she played for an unseen audience.

As Ray listened, tonight wasn't any different. Cari poured

her heart and soul into each note, her heartbreak floating on the summer night's breeze. As the night wore on, she migrated to soft romantic jazz. From his own experience she was working through pain that had nothing to do with wood and plaster. Every person had their own way of coping. Cari was releasing a part of her past that had been taken from her forever.

ALSO BY LUCINDA RACE

The Matchmaker and The Marine May 7, 2020

The MacLellan Sisters

Old and New – June 19, 2019

Borrowed – July 10, 2019

Blue – July 31, 2019

The Loudon Series

Between Here and Heaven – June 2014

Lost and Found – November 2014

The Journey Home – July 2015

The Last First Kiss – November 2015

Ready to Soar – August 2016

Love in the Looking Glass – June 2017

Magic in the Rain – November 2017

STAY IN TOUCH

Thank you for reading my novel. I hope you enjoyed the story. If you did, please help other readers find this book:

- Lend it to a friend you think might like it so she can discover me too.
- Help other people find this book by writing a review.
- Sign up for my newsletter at www.lucindarace.com.
- Like my Facebook page, https:// facebook.com/lucindaraceauthor
- Join Lucinda's Heart Racers Reader Group on Facebook
- Twitter @lucindarace
- Instagram @lucindraceauthor

ABOUT THE AUTHOR

Award winning author, Lucinda Race is a lifelong fan of romantic fiction. As a girl, she spent hours reading novels and dreaming of one day becoming a writer. As life twisted and turned, she found herself writing nonfiction articles, but still longed to turn to her true passion, romance. Now living her dream, she spends every free moment clicking computer keys and has published ten books.

Lucinda lives with her husband Rick and two little pups, Jasper and Griffin, in the rolling hills of Western Massachusetts. Her writing is contemporary, fresh, and engaging.

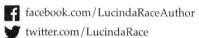

facebook.com/LucindaRaceAuthor
twitter.com/LucindaRace
instagram.com/lucindaraceauthor

Made in the USA
Coppell, TX
20 February 2021